VEGETABLE

GARDEN

Douglas Florian

Voyager Books
Harcourt Brace & Company
San Diego New York London

First voyager books edition 1996
Voyager Books is a registered trademark of
Harcourt Brace & Company.

Library of Congress Cataloging-in-Publication Data
Florian, Douglas.
Vegetable garden / Douglas Florian.—1st ed.
p. cm.
"Voyager Books."
Summary: A family plants a vegetable garden and helps it grow to a rich harvest.
ISBN 0-15-293383-2
ISBN 0-15-201018-1 pb
[1. Gardening—Fiction. 2. Vegetables—Fiction. 3. Stories in rhyme.] I. Title.
PZ8.3F66Ve 1991
[E]—dc20 90-20620

G F E D C

Printed in Singapore

The illustrations in this book were done in pen and ink and watercolor on vellum paper.
The display type was set in Lithos Bold by Thompson Type, San Diego, California.
The text type was set in Cushing Book by Typelink, San Diego, California.
Printed and bound by Tien Wah Press, Singapore
This book was printed on Arctic matte paper.
Production supervision by Warren Wallerstein and Diana Ford
Type design by Lisa Peters

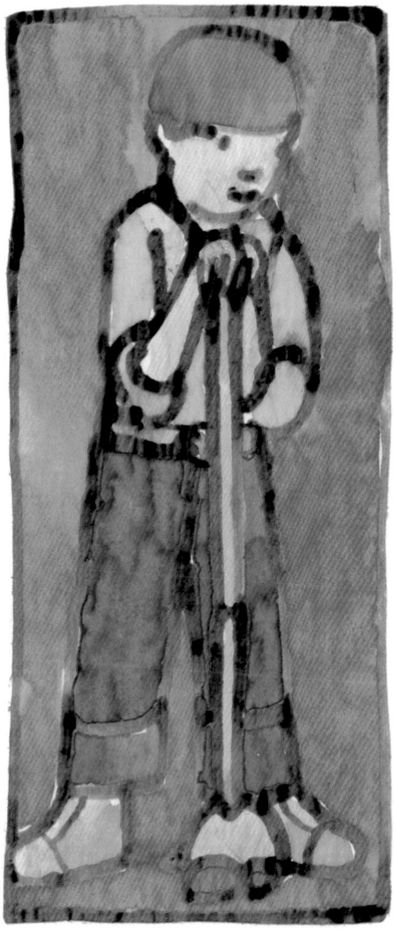

for Yonathan Lallouz

Spade, rake, hoe

Seeds in a row

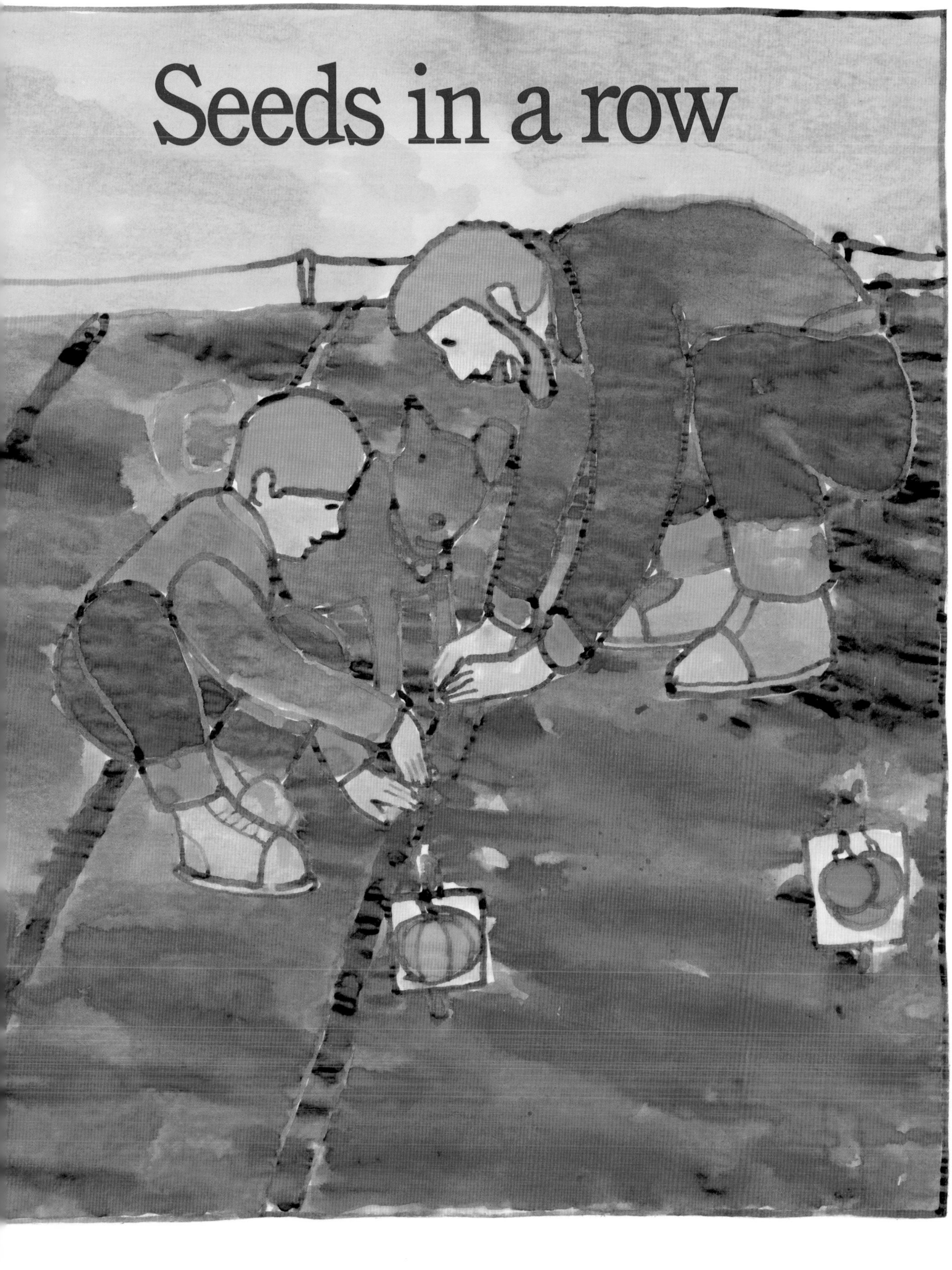

Seedlings sprout

Weeding out

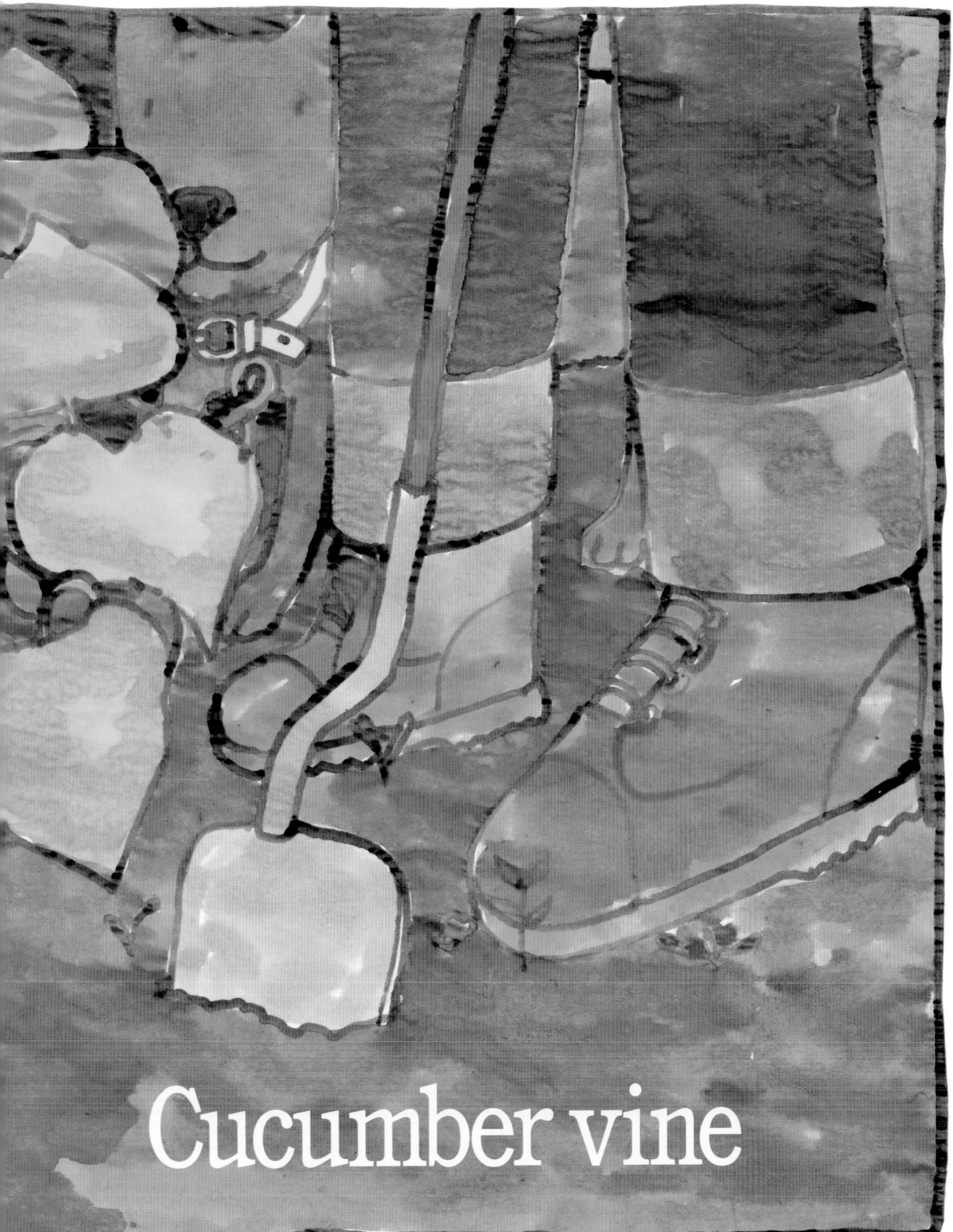

Cucumber vine

Bright sunshine

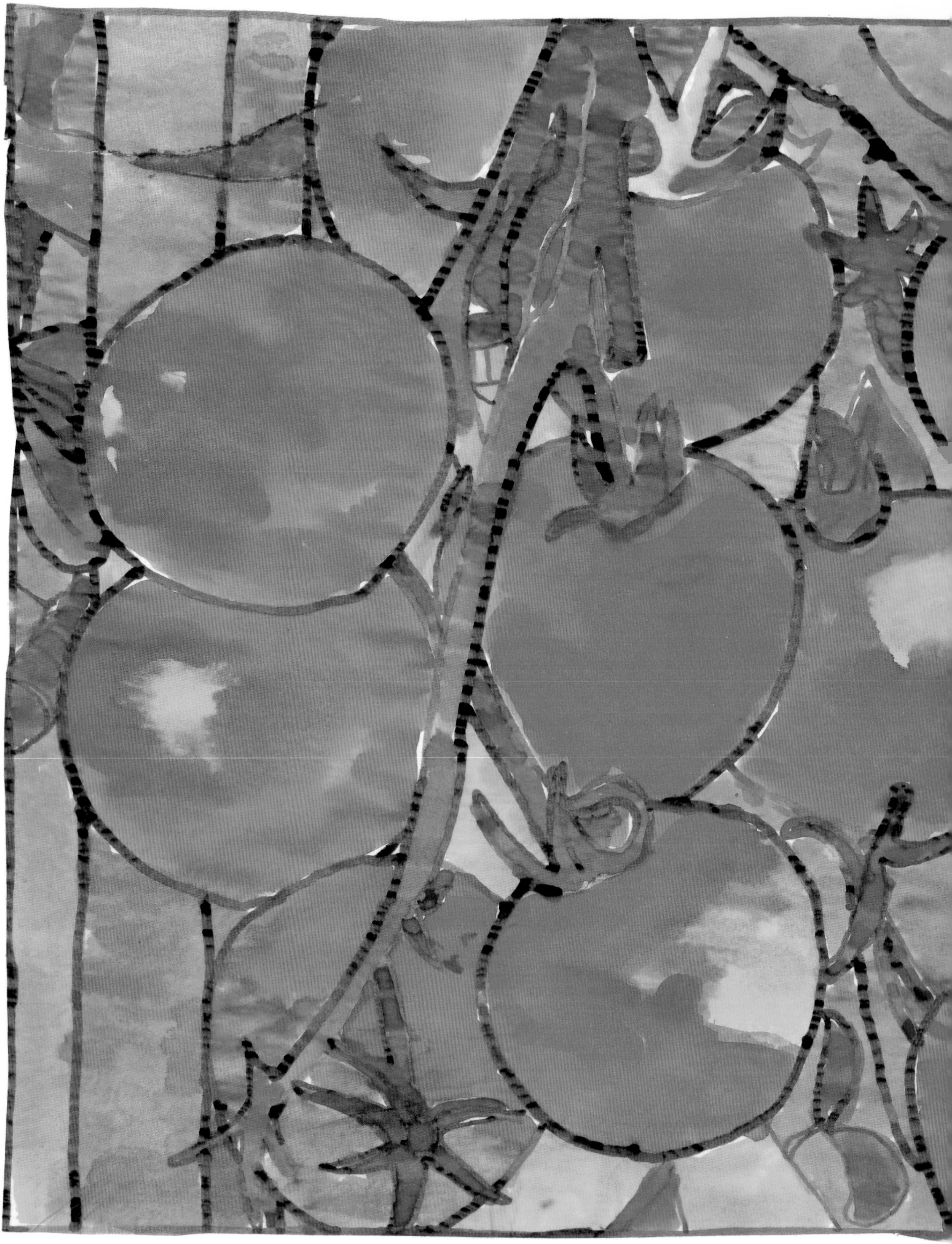

Greens and reds

Lettuce heads

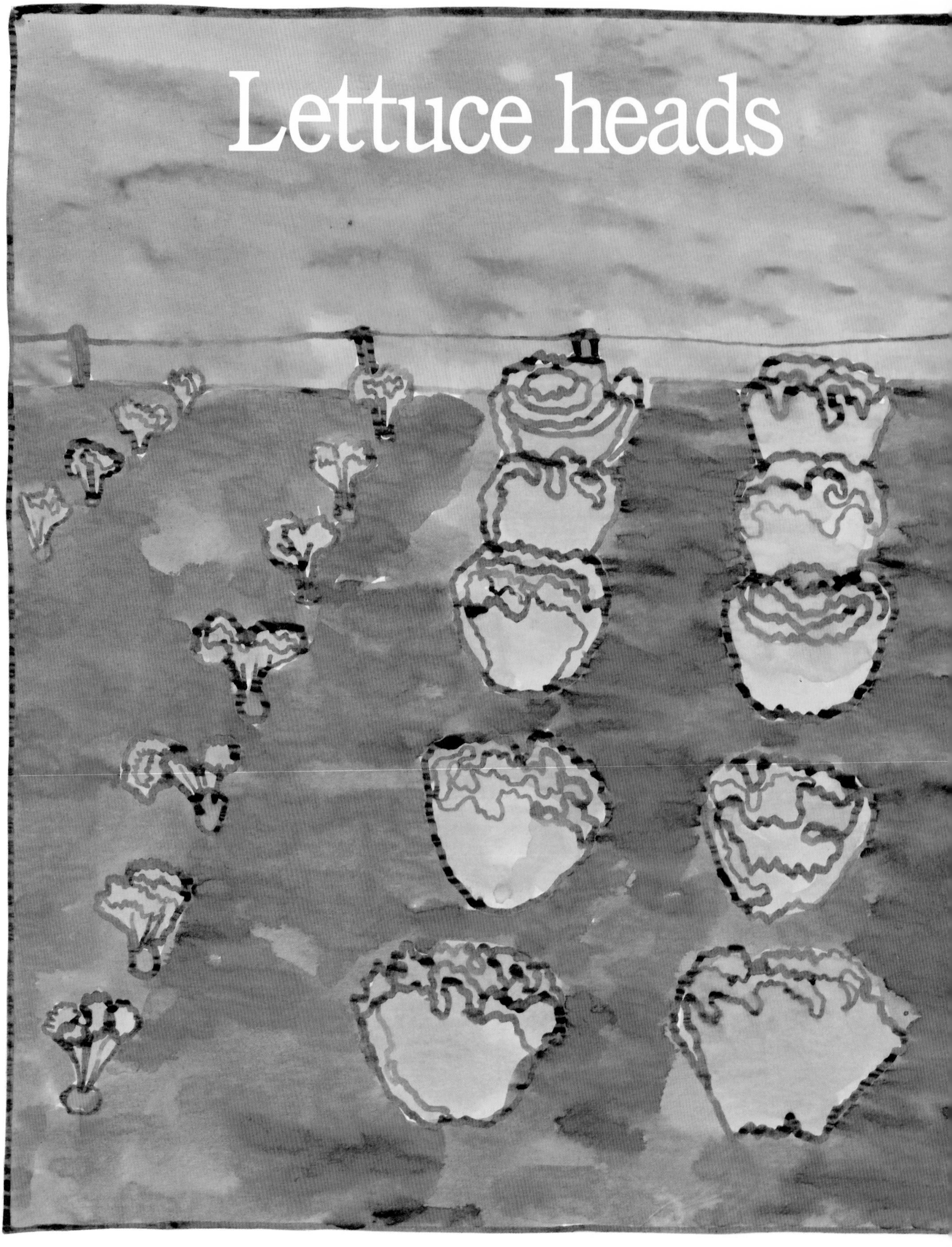

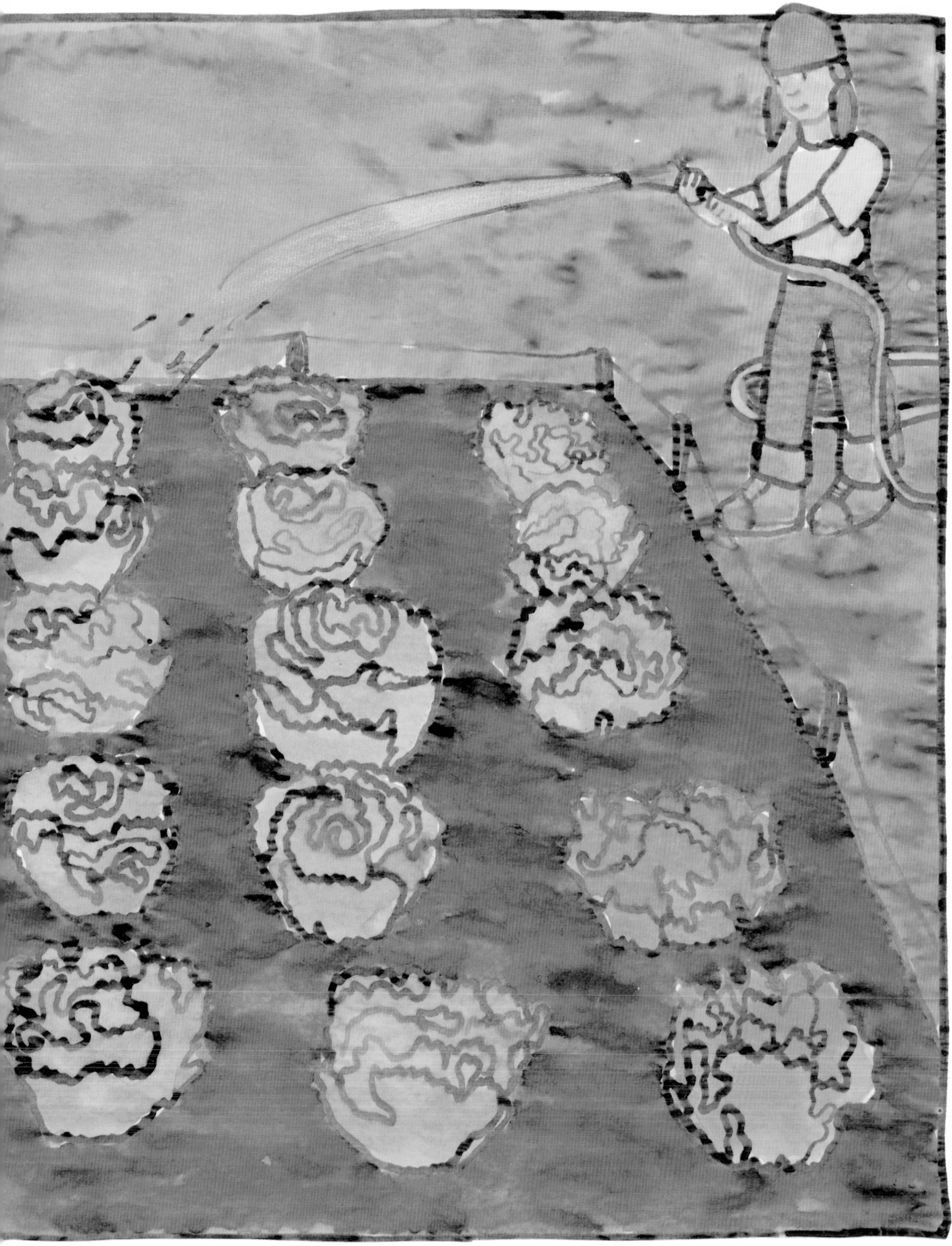

Summer shower

Cauliflower

Big and round

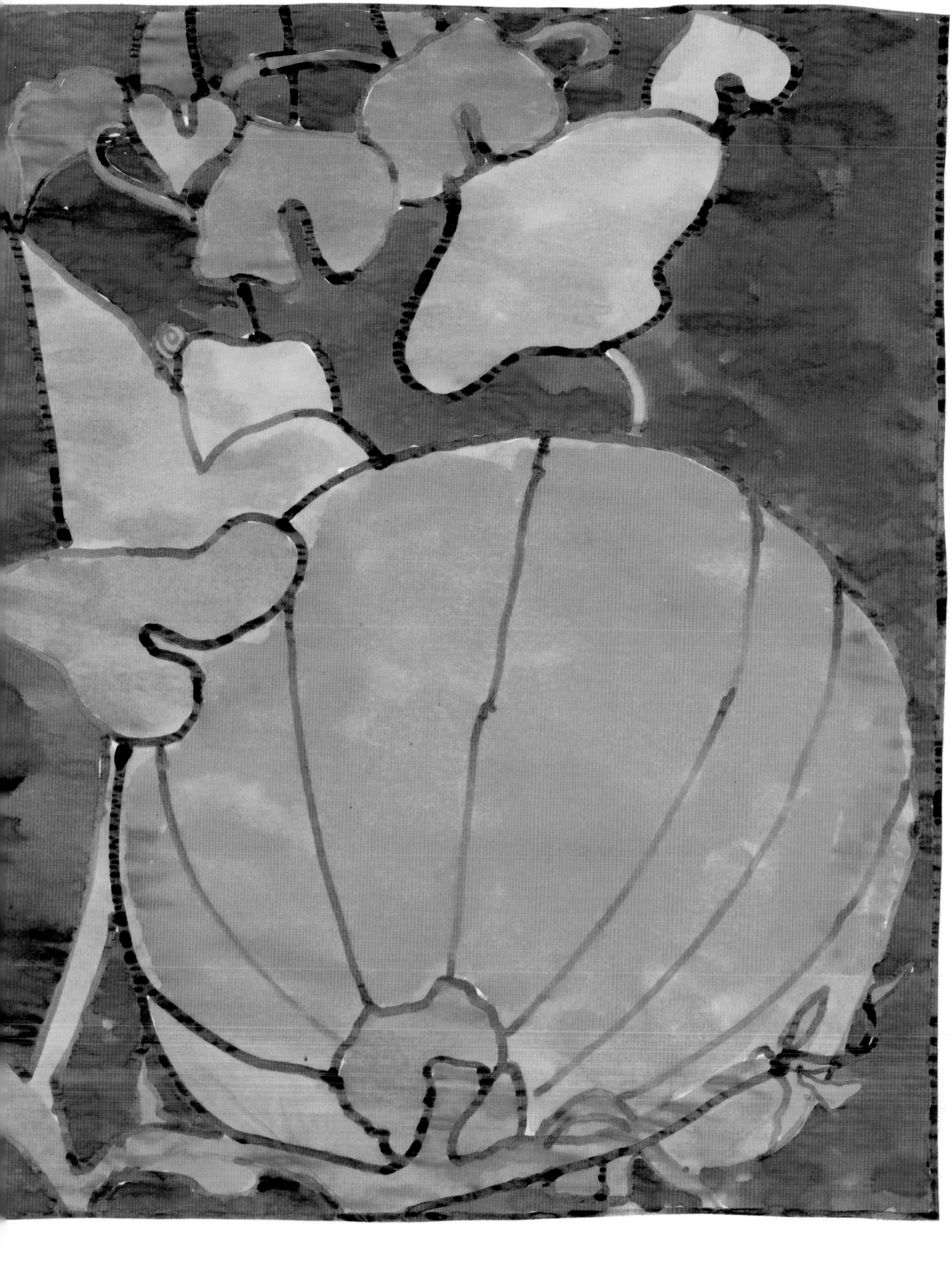

Melon mound

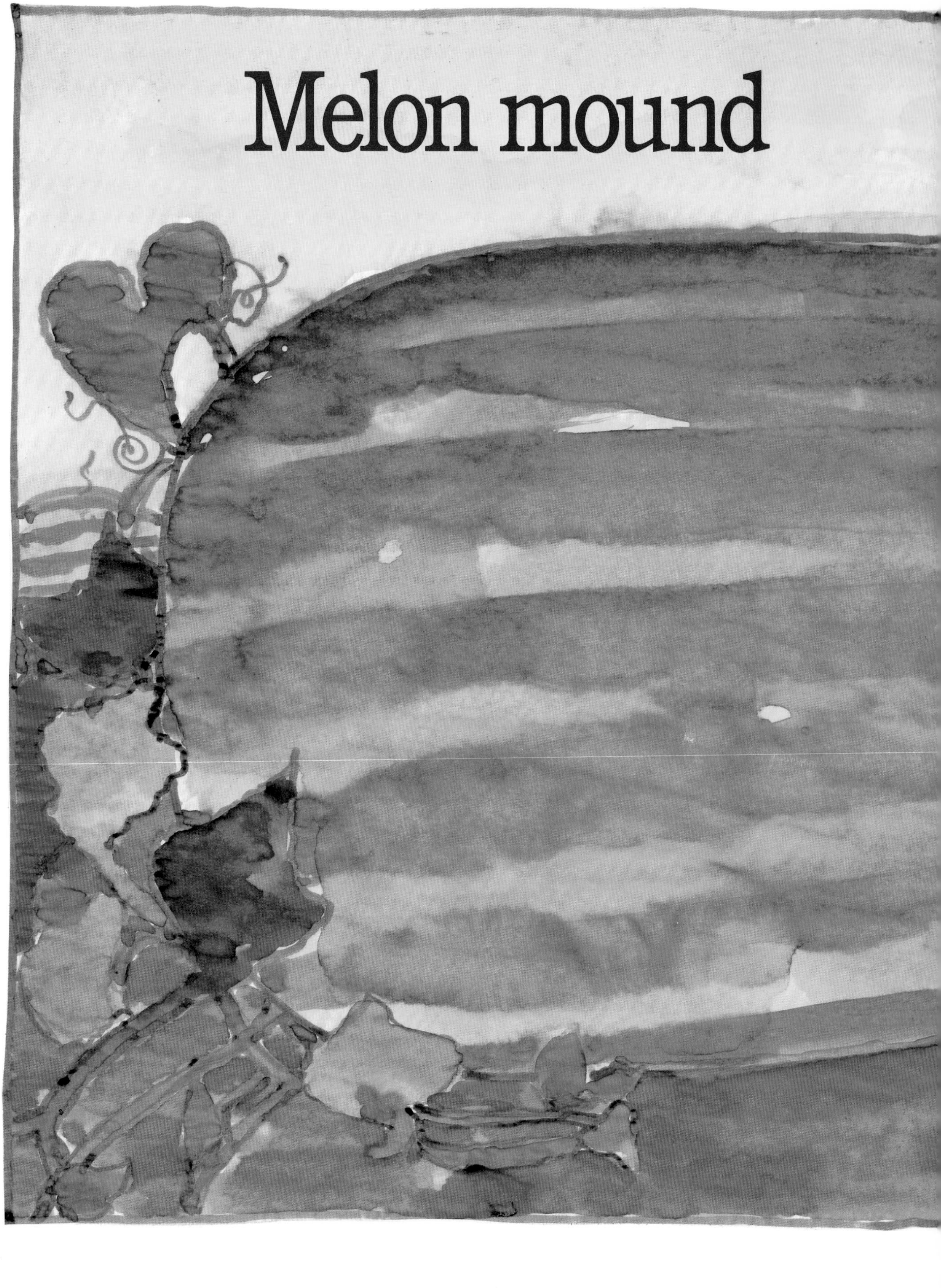

Pea plants climb

Harvest time